3, 2, 1,
Go!

"This is a school zone, Min.
School is hard.
You are not ready."

"Here is the line," said Ann.
"You may not step over it."

"Okay. She is gone.
Now spell *smart*."

Min rolled a rock.

Then she got a board.

"What is Min doing?" said Bess.
"Don't mind her," said Ann.

"Now count
to 100."

Min got a tube and some rope.

The board went
on the rock.
The tube got
a top.

The tube went on the board.

Min took the
rope up
the tree.

She got another rock.

She tied a rope to it.

She pulled.

Min got in.

She put on her helmet.

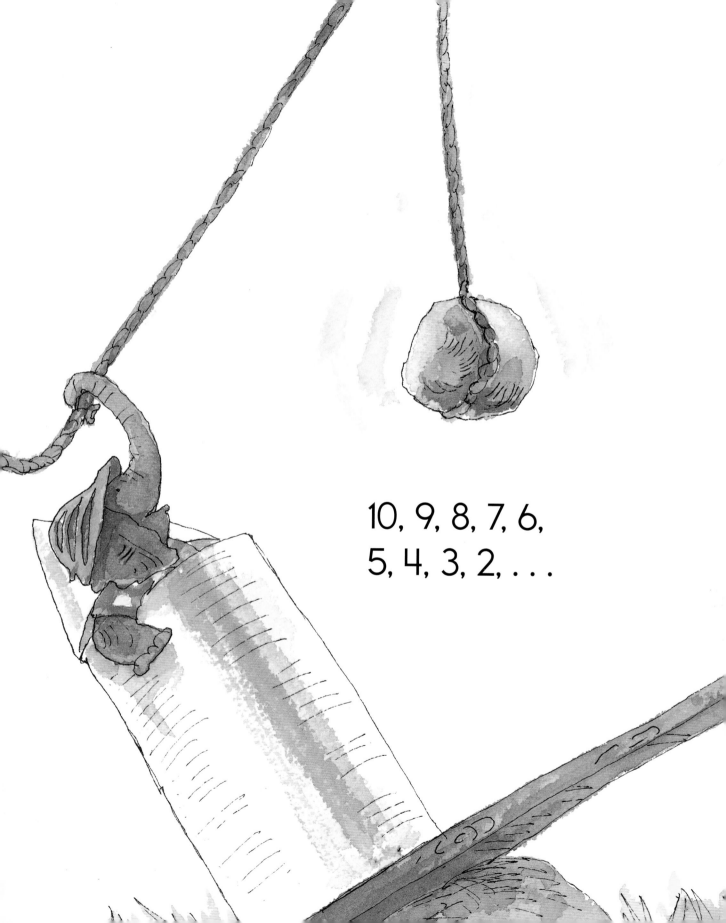

10, 9, 8, 7, 6,
5, 4, 3, 2, . . .

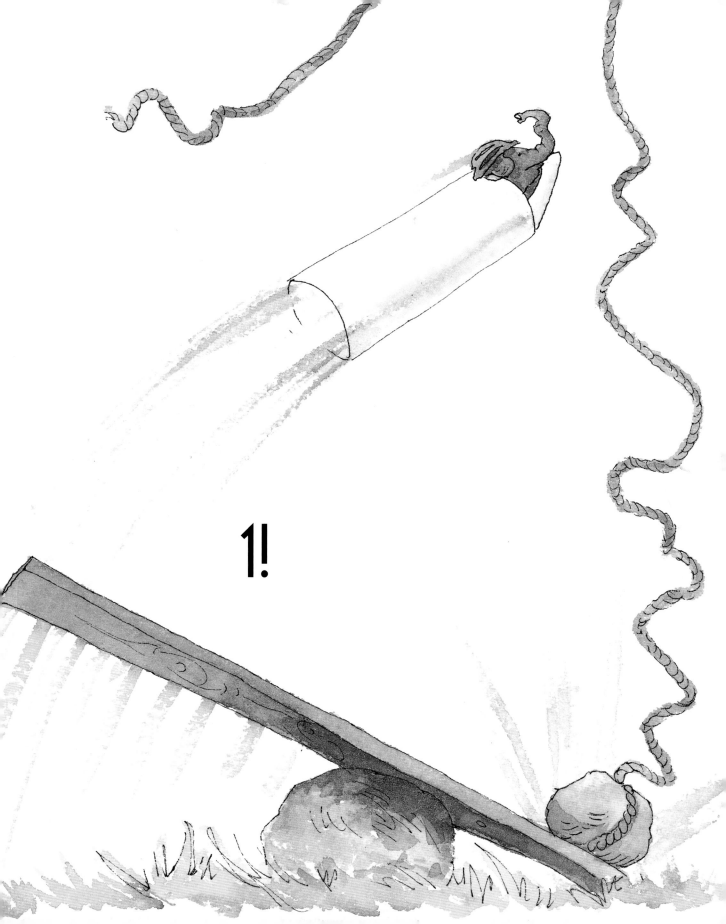

1!

"Here comes Min!" said Bess.

"Hi!" said Min.

"I didn't step over the line.

I flew over it."

"Let's play rocket scientist," said Bess.

You will like these too!

Come Back, Ben *by Ann Hassett and John Hassett*
A KIRKUS REVIEWS BEST BOOK

Dinosaurs Don't, Dinosaurs Do *by Steve Björkman*
A NOTABLE SOCIAL STUDIES TRADE BOOK FOR YOUNG PEOPLE
AN IRA/CBC CHILDREN'S CHOICE

Fish Had a Wish *by Michael Garland*
A KIRKUS REVIEWS BEST BOOK
A TOP 25 CHILDREN'S BOOK LIST BOOK

The Fly Flew In *by David Catrow*
AN IRA/CBC CHILDREN'S CHOICE
MARYLAND BLUE CRAB YOUNG READER AWARD WINNER

Late Nate in a Race *by Emily Arnold McCully*
A BANK STREET COLLEGE BEST CHILDREN'S BOOK OF THE YEAR

Look! *by Ted Lewin*
THE CORRELL BOOK AWARD FOR EXCELLENCE
IN EARLY CHILDHOOD INFORMATIONAL TEXT

Mice on Ice *by Rebecca Emberley and Ed Emberley*
A BANK STREET BEST CHILDREN'S BOOK OF THE YEAR
AN IRA/CBC CHILDREN'S CHOICE

Pig Has a Plan *by Ethan Long*
AN IRA/CBC CHILDREN'S CHOICE

See Me Dig *by Paul Meisel*
A KIRKUS REVIEWS BEST BOOK

See Me Run *by Paul Meisel*
A THEODOR SEUSS GEISEL AWARD HONOR BOOK
AN ALA NOTABLE CHILDREN'S BOOK

You Can Do It! *by Betsy Lewin*
A BANK STREET COLLEGE OUTSTANDING CHILDREN'S BOOK

See more I Like to Read® books.
Go to www.holidayhouse.com/I-Like-to-Read

I Like to Read® Books in Paperback
You will like all of them!

Visit http://www.holidayhouse.com/I-Like-to-Read/ for more about I Like to Read®
books, including flash cards, reproducibles, and the complete list of titles.